ZIG ZAG

The
Disappearing
Cheese

First published 2005
Evans Brothers Limited
2A Portman Mansions
Chiltern St
London W1U 6NR

British Library Cataloguing in Publication Data

Harrison, Paul
        The disappearing cheese. - (Zig zags)
        1. Children's stories - Pictorial works
        I. Title
        823.9'2 [J]

ISBN 0 237 52775 8

Printed in China by WKT Company Limited

Series Editor: Nick Turpin
Design: Robert Walster
Production: Jenny Mulvanny
Series Consultant: Gill Matthews

The Disappearing Cheese

by Paul Harrison
illustrated by Ruth Rivers

Evans

One night a foolish man was
walking past the sea.
His tummy was as empty as
his head.

So when he looked out to sea,
he thought, "My, look at that
cheese under the water.
I'll have that!"

7

He reached out,
but the cheese moved.

He waded into the water,
but the cheese
moved again.

So home he went.

"Wife, come and help me catch a cheese."

But they couldn't catch it.

So home they went.

"Daughter, come and help us catch a cheese."

But still they couldn't catch it.

So home they went.

"Dog, come and help us catch a cheese."

But still they couldn't catch it.

"We need a boat," said
the man.

So off they went to
fetch a boat.

And they chased the cheese
all over the sea...

27

...until a big cloud made
the cheese disappear.

"Ah well," said the man,
"I don't like cheese anyway."

Why not try reading another ZigZag book?

Dinosaur Planet   ISBN 0 237 52793 6
by David Orme and Fabiano Fiorin

Tall Tilly   ISBN 0 237 52794 4
by Jillian Powell and Tim Archbold

Batty Betty's Spells   ISBN 0 237 52795 2
by Hilary Robinson and Belinda Worsley

The Thirsty Moose   ISBN 0 237 52792 8
by David Orme and Mike Gordon

The Clumsy Cow   ISBN 0 237 52790 1
by Julia Moffatt and Lisa Williams

Open Wide!   ISBN 0 237 52791 X
by Julia Moffatt and Anni Axworthy

Too Small   ISBN 0 237 52777 4
by Kay Woodward and Deborah van de Leijgraaf

I Wish I Was An Alien   ISBN 0 237 52776 6
by Vivian French and Lisa Williams

The Disappearing Cheese   ISBN 0 237 52775 8

The Cat in the Coat   ISBN 0 237 52772 3
by Vivian French and Alison Bartlett